Holda and the King of Goose Island

Alison Williams-Bailey

Root and Branch Theatre Company
www.rootandbranchtheatre.co.uk

Artwork by John Wakefield
www.jwakefield.co.uk

First published 2022

ISBN-13: 978-1-7392200-2-0 (eBook)
ISBN-13: 978-1-7392200-0-6 (Paperback)
ISBN-13: 978-1-7392200-1-3 (Hardcover)

Acknowledgements

Many thanks to Partytime and Eva Long Productions for the 'Mother Goose' pantomime which inspired the creation of 'Holda and the King of Goose Island'. I toured in both versions of the 'Mother Goose' and played the Goose and others during the Christmas tours of 2013 and 2017.

Thanks also to William Gallagher of the Writers Guild and FEU who has supported my writing of the book and was the first to give any advice on publication, to Jack Gale, the author of "Holda Queen of Ice and Fire' who I met at Kith of Yggdrasil for his advice on Grimm's writing on Holda, to the Horsham Writers Circle for the first reading out loud and support on publication, and to authors Hugh A. Pryor and Lesley Pardoe for their help and advice. Last but not least, many thanks to Geoff Evans aka Toby Wren for his help with editing and to Danyah Miller, storyteller and editor, who has been one of my most supportive advisors.

Contents

Introduction

Holda and the King of Goose Island tells the story of Pulla's Hill, the pool beside a hill, Pulborough, a village in the heartlands of West Sussex, the land of the South West Saxons. This village wraps itself around a marsh or flat land alongside a river, known as the Brooks, which lies before the chalk hills of the South Downs. This is a mysterious and magical story, for the pool is not a pool, but it is the Arun River also known as the Trisantoris or Trespasser; a name given by the Romans who built a causeway alongside the river.

This story tells how the magical number of *three times passing*, creates the pool that ushers in the "Time between Time," the midwinter season. This is the time when the rain pours and causes the river to flood, making a lake or pool with an island or peninsula. This transforms and changes shape from day to day. The geese and swans and other magical beings live in the otherworldly island in the shadowlands.

Now let us begin at the beginning to find out from where this story finds its origins. Let us then follow the Trespasser on its path from its source in St. Leonard's Forest.

In the Shadow of the Forest

A long time ago a flood engulfed the earth in storms and tempest.

There was a saint who lived in an ancient wood, known as St. Leonard's Forest. He fought a dragon in the woods "where no nightingale would sing, nor no adder sting." St. Leonard killed the dragon and was then reborn as a gift for his heroic act.

Then a spring was born in the woods—the source of the River Arun. It poured out into a stream and flowed through St. Leonard's Forest on a journey all the way to Littlehampton at the mouth of the sea.

The rain poured, flooding the land, and the river grew into a lake. An island was born on the marshland, known as the Brooks. Then the geese on the island made the golden eggs of fertility.

Mother Earth took her sheets which were wet from the floods, she shook them, and they created the snow. The snow settled across the island, the ice covered the lake and the streams. And so it became an island of ice and snow. Then she took her snowshoes to walk across the island between the worlds.

The Mother washed the clothes, drying them out, making strips of clouds in the sky. She took the golden eggs from the geese and put them on the island. Then the eggs bore a giant called Stempo, who wandered across the lands, making the hills and the vales.

For they were the mother and father of the land itself. And it is here that our story begins.

The Making of the Brooks

A long time ago there was a whisper on the wind,
the voice of Gna our messenger friend.
She rides across the galaxy on a beautiful steed,
known as Hopvapnir, Hoof Flourisher.
He gallops and flies over the sky,
while flapping his wings, as the wind does ride.

Gna did whisper and a breeze did blow,
telling the story of dear Stempo.
Then the voice of Gna did whisper and wail.
As a wind it grew, and became a gale.

Stempo was sleeping upon a hill by a pool
when he heard a roar and a thundering sound.
Thunor the Thunderbolt hit the ground.

And a great big dragon known as Knucker the Fiend,
the serpent of the swamp and watery streams,
was fighting a battle with the great Saint Leonard,
as the rain poured over the land.

Then Stempo awoke from the dream
of the battle of St. Leonard and the dragon,
of the streams that flowed out
from the forest of St. Leonards,
and how it grew to make a river over the land.
It was three times passing Trespasser, Arun the river.

So, Stempo marched across the land
stomping on the hills.
Angel Island laughed at the fuss,
for it felt like a twitch or a tickle on the skin.

The chalk in the Hills
traced a sketch on the land.
And the hills grew into a
Down, a Dun Chalk hill.

He stomped and he roared
while the rain poured over
the land, beneath the Down,
and the river flowed all around.

Then he stomped and kicked up his heels,
lifting up his great big foot,
and his old torn shoe
fell onto the ground,
where the Bruc sat under the Down.

Trespasser roared and the Knucker did laugh
while the Angels of the Island were singing.
Then Stempo ran away across the land,
to escape from the bedlam or find a bed,
to rest his tired and sleepy head
and was never seen again.

Bright Elf Beam, the Sun Maiden,
did yawn and fall to sleep.
She dressed the clouds
in shades of pink
and painted the hills adorning the land.

The Huldra folk stepped
out with their pails
to milk the cattle over the Dale.
They hid their tails beneath their dresses.

In the hues of the twilight,
they twisted and turned.
Then danced the dance
of the Dun Chalk Hills,
laughing and singing,
a lullaby of love to the land.

Bright Elf Beam put down her head
on a pillow of clouds
where she lay in a bed.
As the stars did twinkle
and tremor in the sky,
with a giggle and a wiggle,
they laughed and said, "goodnight."

Far in the distance was a long avenue—
a street where the stars do mingle.
Number nine Mrs. Elder Street—
a house in the Milky Way.

There Frau Holle has settled her feet
on the pedal of a spinning wheel,
making the clouds that drift across the sky.

Mrs. Elder, she washed the clothes
and brought the rain to the land.
She shook out her goose feather blanket.
Then the snow fell over the fields.

The Heimchen travel across the land,
with a wagon they follow Mrs. Elder.
She is their foster mother,
they found her in the ice and snow,
beyond the Aurora Borealis,
where the ancestors go to sleep.

Dreaming of their loved ones
they paint the land, with all
the colours of the rainbow.

There in Mrs. Elder Street,
they strapped up the wagon
and peddled their feet.

Crossing the sky, the land, and the sea,
to find an island in the land of dreams,
near the Bruc, the marsh, and the swamp.

They wandered along the Milky Way
to the Aurora Borealis and over
Bifrost the Rainbow Bridge.
Pulling the wagon, sowing
the seeds of life, caught in the breeze.

Mrs. Elder sang a song as they
crossed the swamp,
looking for a home
as the marshlands sunk
over the waters of the flood and the stream.

And there on the Brooks
they did see the shoe of a giant
so tall and wide.
They opened the door to look inside.

"It smells so terrible,"
said Flora, sweetest daughter
of Mrs. Elder's three.

"Well never mind," Mrs. Elder said,
"we can clean and wash.
And sweep and brush,
the dirt away and all the musk."

So the Heimchen, the children,
and Mrs. Elder did work,
until the shoes
turned into a house.
So cosy and warm,
and beautifully dressed in curtains.

Then, singing a song, the Huldra folk
took hold of the plough,
and, dancing, spoke of building
an island out of the swamp
for the angels to live on
as they ploughed all over the land.

And Gna did whisper on the breeze,
"Oh, sing my children
at Sataernalian seed,
for Sataere is bringing
the seed to the land."

A horse, a god, he strides and rides,
over flax and field, bailing the hail
and quelling the storm.
He rode up and strode up,
to Mrs. Elder's house
to bring in the Season of Sataere.

Huldra Song

Here in the hills astraddle the sea
Lies an Etin who's eaten the ground.
He bumps, and he grinds,
He rocks, and he rhymes,
While the little ones circle around.

The cattle are growing
And new life is flowing,
As Nanna is doing her round.

Sing, sing for the hills and the dale,
The valleys that sit neath the fjell.
When Old Mother Hubbard
She looked in her cupboard,
For the fruits and seeds of the land.

There was an old woman
Who lived in a shoe.
She had so many children
She didn't know what to do.
They had no home
Nor a roof for their heads,
Nor broth to eat, nor a bed.

Then the fierce Etin
Straddled the land,
As Trespasser flowed to the sea.
He stomped, and he roared
As a great storm it poured,
In torrents of rain on the breeze.

And the giant he took his great big foot,
And stomped it over the Down.
Then he stomped and he stomped
He raged and he stormed,
As the rains they poured all around.

And being a dance of
The Tempest and storm,
Made the valleys and plains
Near the Down.

And he walked so far, astraddle the hills,
While pressing a plain underground.
They called it a fen or a Brook or a marsh,
For it was plain to see.
The Valley that sits on the edge of the hill
Where the river floats down to the sea.

Trespasser Arun, the giant himself,
Jumped right into the sea
To welcome fair Arun,
The River, the stream,
At the ocean in between.

And as he jumped high over the Downs,
His shoe fell over the fen.
Then the old woman came with her children
And found a roof where the shoe hit the ground.

Sing, sing for the hills and the dales,
The valleys that sit neath the fjell.
When Old Mother Hubbard
She looked in her cupboard,
For the fruits and seeds of the land.

The Old Shoe House

Mrs. Elder and her children
were busy with their work,
planting the seeds
and watering the flowers,
each with a jar and a vessel.

Flora and Daisy, Holly and Ivy,
Bluebell and Tulip,
Polly and Rosemary.
Each had a flower,
a plant to their name,
singing and dancing
and dreaming all day.

Then Mrs. Elder opened
the big front door
to put out the washing
on the line once more.

Then the clouds
traversed the sky,
twisting and turning,
and drifting by and by.

Then a gaggle of geese
flew by, honking like
a rattle and drum.

Ahead of the goose train
was the Old Grey King,
with the White Snow Goose
astride his wing.

The Lady Goose
tripping up was she
flying too low
across the breeze.
And seeing the house
upon the swamp,
she ducked right down, fell then sunk.

While the other geese flew
so high and swift,
she was left by the house,
with nothing to give,
but her goose feather coat
and her wings of the wind.
And so, she knocked on the door.

Inside the house, Mrs. Elder
was weaving and spinning.
The children were shaking out
blankets made of goose feather linen.

And weaving it made
the clouds to grow,
the bed covers
brought in the icy snow.

Then Ivy she opened
the big front door,
where the Lady Goose waited
still clutching at straws.

"Come in Mrs. White Goose.
Let me take your coat."

The snow goose took off
her white feather gown,
as the snowflakes,
twisting and turning,
flew all around.

Then rested on the
floor of the land,
at the Brooks
beneath the Down.

Mrs. Gode, Mrs. Elder's friend,
greeted the children
with sweet amends,
as they sung and laughed
and danced all around.

Hang Out The Washing Song

We peg each piece of cloth
On the rope it will cross,
Here's a peg, here's a peg
Like a peggy, peg leg.

Dingle Dell, Dingle Dell,
We're in the Dingle Dell Valley.
Dingle Dell, Dingle Dell,
We're in the Dingle Dell Valley.
With a peg, a peg, a peggy peg leg.

Mrs. Gode, Mrs. Elder's friend
greeting the children
with sweet amends,
was there to help with the washing.

So they each brought a garment
and she washed it clean,
till the rain began to pour.

And the rain it poured
all day long, then a storm
blew over the land.

Then Bright Elf Beam
knocked on the door.

"I am so very tired.
I am so very sore.
I think it is time for
a few days rest.
Can I sleep on a bed?"

And they all said, "Yes."

So Bright Elf Beam
went to sleep in the bed,
tucked up inside,
while the rain poured
over the ground.

Solstice River Sport

Then in the morning,
while the Sun did sleep,
the children looked out of the door.

There where the river flowed
was a lake or a pool,
and an island had grown
from the rain and the storm.

"Oh look, oh look.
Look out of the door.
There is a lake
and an island
where the river did pour.

The geese they are dancing
all over the land,
on the lake and the river,
where it used to stand."

"Come out my sisters,
brothers and friends,
let us go out onto the lakeside.

Count to ten, five,
six or twenty-three,
play hide-and-seek
beneath the trees," said Flora.

So, the children, the Heimchen,
ran out to the swamp,
wandered down by the river
where the water birds swam.

Hiding in the bushes,
a little bird sang,
of the time between time,
where all life began.

The water was seeping
right up to their knees,
when Flora began
her counting game
with Holly and Ivy, Daisy and Rosemary.

Flora closed her eyes
and counting to ten said,

"One is one and just begun,
Two is who I've found in you,
Three is me and time for tea,
Four is more than I adore,
Five is time to start the jive,
Six is when we pick up sticks,
Seven's eleven we'll find in Heaven,
Eight too late we'll jump the gate,
Nine is fine and just in time."

While the children were hiding
in bushel and briar,
Flora walked down to the bank.

A little duck chirped
"Look out," said he
"step away, step away."

For she stooped too
close to the water.

And sitting on the branch
of a great ash tree,
she dipped her toe in the water.

Aske the ash, was the father of men,
he told her an old story
of the time when
the waters did flood
across the land,
and Noah did ride on the Ark.

As he spoke, Flora
began to dream
and she gazed
at the reflections
upon the stream,
of water that bubbled and swirled.

Mrs. Elder picked up the spindle
in the old shoe house
and wove the webs of the blanket
to help Bright Elf Beam
in her sleeping time and
she sang a song as she worked.

Then the clouds did
float across the sky,
as Bright Elf Beam,
still sleeping, smiled
and little lights fell out on the water.

Then up jumped a fish,
a toad, or an eel,
and a face peered
out of the water.

It giggled then dipped down,
under the stream
and a tail disappeared underneath.

Flora, she gazed as
the clouds floated by
into the swirling waters.
And saw the pictures
upon the edge,
the mirror of life itself.

Underwater World
in the time between time,
revealed its truth
in the lights upon the water.

Then the Naiade poked up
its head once more,
and spoke to Flora.
"Hello," it said.

Flora jumped and grabbed
onto the branch,
nearly falling into the lake.

"Who's there?" she said,
alarmed and confused.

"Don't worry, I'm Nixen, your friend.
I have come to help you
get over the stream.
To return to where
you came from,
in the passage in-between."

Flora said,
"Oh hello. I didn't see you.
What is a Nixen?
And who are you?
Oh, sorry Nixen, it is your name.

I would love to join your adventure.
But I have my duties,
to help my mother,
brothers, sisters, and friends."

Nixen replied saying,
"If you wish to help
Mrs. Elder and folk,
come follow me now,
in the stream we will float
beyond the seas."

Then the Nixen disappeared
under the stream
and Flora tried to catch him
before he did leave.

Then she fell off the branch,
into the well,
at the Time of Chance.

For at the foot of the
Great Ash Tree,
was the Well of Urd
of all mysteries.

As Flora fell all the way down
she called out,
"Nixen, where are you?"

Then she found herself
back in her bed and
tossed off her covers
from her sleepy head.

"Mother, oh, Mother.
I have woken at last.
Did you go to the island?
Did you do the dance?"

But there in the place
of her sisters and friends,
was a beautiful lady
all dressed in white,
with a veil and a staff
and a stalactite.

"Where am I?" said Flora.
And the lady smiled.

Hide and Seek for Flora

Now let us now return
to the children
who were playing,
looking for Flora
and believing she was lost,
were worried and scared
and counting the cost.

"Flora, oh, Flora.
We've lost her," they cried.

"Let us run back to Mother.
She will help us find
our dear sister Flora.
Oh, where can she be?
Let us go back to the house,
the old torn shoe.
Dear Mother will help us,
it is all that we can do."

So, Ivy and Holly,
Daisy and Rosemary,
ran to the house,
feeling quite dotty.
Dozy or dippy,
dandling the Dell,
in the valley before the Down.

"Mother, oh Mother.
We have lost Flora!" They cried.

"Near the river
beside the creek.
Where we were playing
hide and seek."

Then Mother replied saying,

"What do you mean?
You played by the lake?
The water is growing,
and it is not safe
to play so close to the edge.

Oh, never mind, children
we will go out and see
if Flora has hidden
or decided to play
with the Geese or the swans
who are dancing away."

So, Mother and the children
strode out to the lake
on the edge of the island
where they looked for Flora.

The sweetest child,
who cared for her foster
mother, sisters, and friends;
for whom the light
would never end,
which shone from her sweet aura.

Then looking across
the watery stream.
They heard a strange voice
upon the breeze,
singing the song of Trisantoris.

There was a great sailboat,
upon the seas, with a
dragon helm it did row.
Where little fairy lights
flickered out from its bough,
floating through the mist upon the water.

Mrs. Elder and the children
gazed out over the lake
as the boat drew closer and closer.

A great serpent dragon
was swimming with the tide,
propelled by the Nixen,
water fairy of the stream.
Then a seal jumped up
and poked his head out of the water.

Ivy and Holly were so enthralled,
they put their hands out
to stroke it and all.
The children called out,
so excited to see a seal
leap out of the water
and onto the boat.

Mrs. Elder and the children
were shocked and alarmed,
then laughed at the wondrous display.

Mrs. Elder said,
"Oh, I jumped out of my skin."

"No, that is what he did!"

The children said laughing,
as the boat pulled onto the bank.

There was a great man
dressed in the robes
of a Lord, who spoke, saying,

"Welcome, I am Heimdall,
the Selkie, half seal, half man
and Lord of Underwater World.

I am here with the Naiad,
the Nixen, and Knucker,
to take you over to Goose Island
and help you find Flora,
the Heimchen maid."

Then the Naiad sang as
they rowed over the water

The Nixe Song

Come and see the magic land,
The tale of twixt and tween,
In our home on Goose Island,
We'll stir the land of dreams.

Even every day we learn
To flourish and to grow.
Just a little way between
The wind, the rain, the snow.

Here we come to Goose Island
To measure and to mow.
Sing a song of when we worked
To wax and wane and sow

Even every day we learn
To flourish and to grow.
Just a little way between
The wind, the rain, the snow.

Mrs. Elder and the Heimchen
were helped onto the boat,
then taken across to the island.

The dragon turned
and floated away,
twisting and turning
upon the breeze.

It waved to the children
as they began to leave.
Mrs. Elder, she waved
and called "farewell."

Then the little ones turned
to see the Nixe
jump and twist
and turn in the water,

As the dragon disappeared
from sight and sound.

Moss Maidens' Wood

High on the bank was
a grove of trees.
With twigs and branches,
floating on the breeze.
They seemed to wave
and say "hello,"
with smiling faces
in the undergrowth.

Then a wind whipped up
and stirred the leaves,
as they fell all around
from under the trees.

The children walked out
into the woods,
a deep dark forest
from where they stood,
holding hands, they followed the path.

And as they walked past
the mossy banks,
the snow fell down
from the branches,
and leaves and twigs of the trees.

The Moss Maidens were
singing a song
and dancing along.

The Heimchen walked by
hand in hand.

"Oh mother," they cried,
"It has begun to snow,
we are lost in the forest
with nowhere to go."

Mrs. Elder she spoke to
the trees all around,

"Hello, who are you?
Such a pretty song.
What incites you to sing
this beautiful throng?"
Then the Moss Maidens replied,

"We are the Moss Maidens.
We bring in the snow
from the dying leaves,
that reap and sow."

Then a gentle wind
blew across the trees.
Snowflakes were swirling
and twisting in the breeze,
dancing all around.

The children ran over
to catch the snow.
Dancing, running,
and skipping to and fro.

There in the distance
was a tall slim tree.
Reaching as high
as the sky in-between
the horizon and the sleeping
Sweet Bright Elf Beam.

The sleeping giant
had a fine silver trunk,
with beams that hung over
the Moss Maidens' dance.
And a face that hid in
the shade of a branch.

The children attempted
to climb up and see,
the beautiful picture
of the snow lined trees,

And felt a shudder
as they climbed
from branch to beam.

Then the Elm she
opened her eyes
and seeing the children
was mesmerised.

She giggled and wiggled
as she opened her mouth,
to speak the fine words
of the Elm of Chance.

"Hello there, dear little ones.
What brings you into my lair?
Will you build a nest on
my branches and beams?
The bough is my home
where I welcome thee."

The children, so startled,
fell straight to the ground.
What on earth was this creature
with the speech so profound?

There resting by
the roots of the tree
was an old Corn Dolly
and asleep was he till
the break of the day,
dressed in a coat
like a bale of hay.

It was Sir Sceafing,
the last of the Corn.
The Grain of the harvest
from which he was born.

For the tree was no less
than Embla the Elm.
The mother of all trees,
of women and men.

The Wild Hunt

The House of Odin
led the Wild Hunt—
pulling the wagon,
riding the sky,
with Mr. and Mrs. Woden, by and by.

"Bellow, bellow,"
sounded the horn.
Hugin and Munin
in the wind were torn.

Flapping their wings,
they flew into the woods,
and settled on a branch
where together they stood.

Then a howling wind
blew across the trees
as the Moss Maidens shivered,
and Gna did gallop and circle around.

A pack of hounds were
pulling the cart,
stumbling and tumbling
beneath the Elm of Chance.

Then Sleipnir appeared from
out of the shade.
The eight-legged beast
he did behave.

He had come for a snack,
to eat some porridge.
The last of the corn,
the Gruelsome grain
and visit Mr. Sceaf, his friend.

34

"Hello Sleipnir.
Are you here for a feast?"

"I have been hunting and howling
all over the sky,
to bring in the season,
by and by," Sleipnir said in reply.

Then Hugin and Munin
did begin to crow.
A bellowing sound did
shake the ground,
till the icicles were
shattered and torn.

Then the Moss Maidens
turned in their sleep.

Sceaf said to Hugin,
"Hello Hugin. Tell me
what is on your mind?"

Hugin told him,
"I think that
Mr. and Mrs. Woden
are close behind."

"Hello Munin.
Do you remember
the last time we spoke?"

"It was in the arms of
the great big oak,
Yggdrasil the World tree.
But here comes
Mr. and Mrs. Woden
out on the breeze," said Munin.

Sleipnir was munching
and chewing the grain.
The children were skipping
and dancing in train.

The children saw him,
So they said,
"Hello Mr Horse.
Please tell us your name?"

"I am Sleipnir, the eight-legged
horse of Odin. I ride the Wild Hunt
that is here again—
to bring in the season
of Yuletide games."

Then a howl and a giggle
caused a shiver through
the trunks of the beech and the elm.

As crashing through the air
a wagon did hurl
with howls of laughter
that did unfurl.

Geri and Freki, the
Wolf Dogs of Woden
leaped into the woods.
Just in time to miss
the great calamitous crash
of Woden's wagon, upon the path.

The children were playing
with Sleipnir and his friends,
Hugin, Munin, and Gna.

Mr. and Mrs. Woden
crawled out in shock,
laughing and mocking each other.

Mrs. Elder was sitting with Mr. Sceaf.
Then jumped up
to rescue the couple,
as they stumbled out from
the cart now torn to pieces.

Mrs. Woden greeted
the crowd saying,

"Greetings fair maidens,
mystery friends.
What brings you to Embla
in the forest of the Shadow Realm?"

Then Moss Maidens said,

"Hello Mrs. Woden.
We are sorry to see
such a terrible mishap.
We are coming to
help you at last.

We have made the snow
across the land—
to bring in the season,
to help with your ride,
to decorate Embla from Earth to Sky."

Mrs. Woden replied,

"Well you were a little late,
so, we set off anyway.
Over the fields,
the horse and the hay.

But the wagon has broken,
the axle is torn.
Oh, goodness, I do feel
so quite forlorn."

Mrs. Elder stepped forward
with an urge to help
Mr. and Mrs. Woden,

"Greetings, may I introduce myself
and my infant train.
I am Mrs. Elder."

Mr. Woden then said,

"The Milky way?!
Oh, goodness you have
travelled so far!"

"Yes, I've walked along
the Milky Way over
the Aurora Borealis.
Then I crossed the line
of the Rainbow Bridge,"
said Mrs. Elder.

Mrs. Woden replied,

"Well greetings,
so, good to meet you.
I think we have lost our way.

Our wagon is broken,
at the break of the day.
The Sun Disc is sleeping,
the horizon is torn.
But who are these
delightful children?"

Then Holly and Ivy, Poppy,
Daisy and Rose said,

"Can we help with the wagon?
We can fix it we know."

Embla coughed and
wiggled her trunk,
as she shivered and
shook in the breeze.

Then a branch of
the tree fell down
over Mrs. Elder.

"Do you mind Mrs. Elm,"
she said shocked and alarmed.

"My name is Embla. I am
the mother of mankind
and of all the people on Earth."

So, Mrs. Elder replied,

"Well thank you Dear Mother,
but that really did hurt.
Could you please take care,
when you drop your
branches and twigs
upon the ground."

Then Embla she sang a beautiful song.
Twisting and turning,
the Moss Maidens danced along.

Whipping up the snow,
surrounding the tree.
The many branches, leaves,
and twigs fell onto the ground.

The children were amazed
by the sounds of choral harmony,
that thrilled the air.

They picked up each branch
then stood in line,
to gift the Wodens
for their Wagon in time.

To send the Wild Hunt
back over the land,
bringing presents and
gifts for every man.

Mrs. Woden picked up
the branches and put
them in a stack.

"Oh dear," she said.
"I really do not know
how to fix them and
put them back together."

So Daisy took off her sock
and gave it to Mr. Woden.

"It has got so wet with the
Moss Maidens' snow.
You might as well use it,
then off we will go."

Mr. Woden said,

"Well thank you kind maiden
and what is your name?"

"I am Daisy.
I water the flowers
after which I was named."

Then the other children
took off their socks.
Their gloves, their scarves,
whatever they had got—
to help fasten the branches
into an axle and fix the wagon.

Mr. Woden said,
"Thank you, kind children,
Mrs. Elder and Embla.
You have helped us
fix the wagon.

Now we must be off
in this westerly breeze,
for the season is waiting
to bring in fate and destiny."

Mrs. Woden called out,

"Hugin and Munin, Sleipnir,
Geri and Freki,
troops and all.
Let us fasten the wagon
and begin the thrall.

Get out your trumpets,
as our hounds do howl.
It is night-time and
the right-time for
our seasonal travel.

Over the hills,
the fields and the dales,
bringing gifts to all
the sleeping children.
We say fare thee well,
adieu, now off we go."

Then the Wild Hunt galloped away
with the howling hounds.
They drove into the air, flying so high.

Christmas Morning

Then Embla did open
a door in her trunk,
as the children made
a bed on the moss.

The little ones rested
safe and warm,
in the bough of the ancient tree.

The snowdrops made a blanket
over the ground,
where the children did
delve in their dreams.

Until at the break of the day,
a cockerel did crow,
and the crow did call
"Cock-a-doodle-do" crow sound.

Ivy jumped up looking at her foot.
"Ouch, what is sticking
on the end of my sock?"

Holly said, "Your foot has
grown so huge!"

"Holly, be nice to Ivy."
Mother said to the maids,
with a chorus of giggles and glee.

Then Ivy took off the sock
from her foot
and gold coins
fell to the ground.

Then Holly said,
"Ouch, something is
sticking on my foot.
It weighs a hundred pounds."

Holly pulled off her sock
and a golden egg
hit the ground.

It bounced into the air
and circled around,
then fell into the roots of the tree.

Embla laughed
as her branches
shook in the breeze.

"A present on this
Yuletide morn.
A gift for a gift as
the New Year is born.

For you gave your help
to the Woden's Wild Hunt.
So they may bring gifts
to children, all over the land."

Bluebell chuckled saying
"But not to the naughty ones."

"Yes, to those, helpful,
loving and kind,
like Holly and Ivy.
Let us name Christmas after you.

For you have helped bring in
the Yuletide Morn,
helping the hounds
of the Wild Hunt.
Let us sing and Hail the Day."
Embla spoke to all around.

So, the children and Mother
shook out the bedding,
and the snow began to fall.

Then they danced and sang
a Yuletide song:
"Snowflakes Are Falling On My Head."

Embla made a picnic of acorn and corn
to break the fast
as the children sang:

"Oh, Christmas Tree.
Oh, Christmas Tree.
How lovely are your branches."

To Embla the Mother of all
the trees, on the birth of the Sun
and the dawn of the year.

Then they packed up
and sacked up
their clothing and socks,
and said goodbye to
the elderly tree,
with a kiss and a hug.

Her eyes they closed
as she fell to sleep,
for another year
and her work was done.

The Heimchen started their journey
out of the woods.
And there on the ground,
marking the path,
were footprints
in the shape of a bird.

Then a honking sound
was caught on the breeze,
as the wings did rustle up,
the leaves of the trees.

High overhead
was a line of geese
in the form of an arrow.

Tyr and Tuisto
the Gods of the sky.
Ensued the battle,
to bring new life
to the ground.

Bluebell said, "Listen Mother,
the Wild Hunt is winging.
They have come back
to see us again."

The children rushed to jump up
and wave their hands
to all their friends.

But only the geese were flying
in the sky, high up into
the mountainside,
as the mystery magic ensued.

Mother said, "Come along children.
Let us follow the footprints,
as the goose do fly.
We will climb the Crystal Mountain,
into the sky and look
for our fair Flora."

So, the Heimchen and Mother
climbed into the hills,
over the dales,
the Mystery Miles,
on a journey to find their friends.

The Cave on the Mountain

In a cave on the mountain
young Flora did sleep,
dreaming of destiny days.

Falling so deep into the well,
the voices rang out,
like a magical spell.

"Flora, oh Flora,
now wakey, wakey."

Then Flora awoke in
a deep dark cave,
with a beautiful fountain.
It was paved with
stalagmites and stalactites.

Standing overhead was
a fine young woman,
dressed in gold
with a veil of silver.

She was singing a song
as she sat at her work.
Spinning and weaving
as the time unfurled.

Singing the song of
destiny's dawn,
the chorus of the birth of the Sun.

As Flora awoke
she rolled over
and found her skirt
gathered up to her knees.

Revealing there hidden
the large, webbed shaped foot,
she kept hidden, from all to see.

"Where am I?"
She cried out
in shock and despair,
"Oh no, my foot!"

She was alarmed to see
her webbed foot
naked and bare.

She covered it over,
pulled down her skirt,
the blankets and sheets of her bed.

The lady she laughed
with a gentle sound,
like music or birdsong,
a harp, or a lyre,
as she smiled and
stuck out her foot.

"Who are you?"
said Flora.

"I am the White Lady.
Bertha, the Goose footed
Queen of Goose Island,
your Fairy Godmother.

Here, let me show you.
This is the Elf foot and Goblin's cross.

I am the Queen of Snow Mountain
and this is my cave,
where the fountain Quickborn
brings destiny's day.

We of the Elfen kind
have brought you here,
an unbaptised child,
born of the royal Gosling line,
Princess of Goose Island."

Flora was shocked, stunned,
and speechless in thrall.
As the elf folk appeared
and dressed her in gold.

"Are you really
my Godmother?
Where is Holda, my Mother, the Heimchen,
My family and friends?
From whom I am torn
and lost without end."

Bertha said,
"Mrs. Elder adopted you
just after you were born.
But you are an elf maiden
of the Gosling Line.

So we ushered you in,
like a voice on the breeze.
To cross through the well,
in the passageway between time
to Aelfheim and Crystal Mountain.

Now let me show you
how spinning can make
the elf foot grow."

So, they spun,
and they wove,
as the time did grow.

For Flora did fall into
the Well of Chance,
up into Quickborn,
the Fountain of Youth
in a seasonal dance.

To usher in Yuletide,
as the Heimchen did call
and seek for her over the bank.

Heimdall, the White God,
his horn did sound,
then Bertha picked up
the bucket and pail
saying to Flora,

"Come my young one.
To the mountain we will go,
to milk the cattle and the field to sow."

Crystal Mountain Snowfell

High on the hills
Bertha did stride
with Flora and milk pail beside her.

Dressed in grey
they followed the path
that led to the top of Snowfell;

the Crystal Mountain
that sits in the clouds,
hidden from Midgarden.

Flora followed the Lady
all the way up the path,
as the cattle did moo and call.

Then a strange sweet sound
echoed in the glen,
as the Huldra hid deep in the hills.

Singing a song
to call in the cattle,
as they danced all over the ground.

Laughing and singing,
they milked the cows.
Then over the horizon
Audhumla came—the cow
that gave life to all
beings on Earth.

Audhumla said to all,

"It is Mother's Night,
that brings in the
birth of the Sun;
Merry Solstice and a
Happy New Year to all."

A howling and baying of
hounds did cry,
over the crest of the hill.
The Wild Hunt flew,
and the geese did honk.

Mr. and Mrs. Woden rode
on Sleipnir astride,
as the eight-legged horse
ushered in Yuletide.

A wagon came crashing
over the edge,
pulled by Sleipnir
the eight-legged horse.

To bring the Heimchen
and Mother at last,
to find Flora here in the hills.

Flora then ran
to greet them all
with love and hugs abound.

The geese they honked,
the sound of the horn,
of the Wild Hunt of Woden's kind.

They flew like the arrow
of Tuisto and Tyr,
the sky god of ancient times.

Bertha greeted Mrs. Elder
there on the fjell
and asked her
how she came to
fly with the Wodens,
Kingly Lord and Lady of Aelfheim.

Mother told her,

"Well that is a long story;
we followed the footprints in the snow,
the Elf Cross and Goblin's Foot.

We walked over the island
as a great snow did pour
and the wind did roar.
While the geese were
honking and flying so high.

Mr. and Mrs. Woden
in the wagon did ride.
They stopped and
offered us a lift inside.

So then we rode
over the lands,
sending gifts to the children
asleep in their beds,
dreaming of Santa Claus."

Bertha she smiled and said,
"Well you have come in time
for the Yuletide feast.
Let us celebrate, dance,
sing and eat."

Then Bertha took up
her spindle staff
and held it high in the air.

She sang a song to the cattle,
to usher in
The Time Between Time.

Then a door slid open
in the side of the hill,
to reveal the Crystal Cave.
Then all the revellers
they entered in and
began to misbehave.

Standing at the door
stood the Old Grey King,
Lord of the Gosling line.
Greeting all and sundry
who came to celebrate
the Season of Solstice Time.

Sataere's Grotto known also as Santa's Grotto

"Welcome and greetings,"
said the old Grey King,
as the train of misrule entered in.

The stalagmites and stalactites
glittered and shimmered
with a rainbow of colours on the pool.

The children, the Heimchen, ran inside
to play hide and seek,
mystified by the fountain Quickborn,
the beautiful spring
where the geese and the swans did swim.

The Huldra folk were dancing
and singing a song,
as the elder folk
entered the cave.

The Wodens with Sleipnir came galloping in.
Geri and Freki did howl.
Then Hugin and Munin
fluttered around,
as a great horn blew a sweet sound.

Heimdall stepped out
from the bridge,
as Bifrost opened its door.

Then the Huldra and the Lady
both stepped forth,
into the Cavern of Yuletide.

"Greetings to all,
at Mother's Eve.
We bring our spindles forth.

I am Bertha the White Lady.
I have the flax
a foliage for you,
and the mystery stones
from the mountain and moor.

I leave it to you to choose.
The flax blue flowers
bring love to the land,
and the stones
bring riches and more."

Then each took their turn
to choose in line,
a flax for the fields
or a stone for the hearth.
The spinning with
spindles commenced.

Flora and Daisy
played by the well,
as the geese swam
onto the lake.

They both sang a song
and chanted a rhyme
for Christmas time.

Daisy saw Flora's large,
web-shaped foot
and said; "Oh, what is that?"

And Flora she told her,
"It is my web-shaped foot.
For I was adopted
when I was born,
by our mother, Mrs. Elder.

Bertha the White Lady
is my birth mother,
Queen of the Gosling line.

I fell through the well
by the river tree
to return to my family home."

Daisy, she laughed and said,

"Oh, Flora you tell such tales.
Come let us go and
do the spinning,
for the contest has now begun."

So they danced and waltzed
across the cave,
to join the spinning line.
And they both took the flax
as their choice of gift.

Then Mrs. Elder spoke
to Bertha at last,
"Please tell me how Flora came here?"

Bertha said, "Here let me show you
my web-shaped foot.
I am Gosling of the royal line.
And this is my elf foot,
Elf cross and Goblin Foot.
For we are of the Elfin Kind.

Flora is a princess
and I am her mother.
Mrs. Elder you have been so kind.

Thank you for rescuing
my daughter sweet Flora
to bring her up safe and warm.

In the house on the Bruc
made from a shoe,
with the Heimchen, the children,
her brothers and sisters.

For now, it is time
that she shall inherit
her royal birth right
to follow the Gosling line."

Mrs. Elder she smiled,
then they both embraced
and drank a toast
to the elderly folk,
the Disir who brought in Yuletide.

Then Bertha said,
"Children, the Heimchen
and Huldra folk,
bring out the harp and the horn.

For I have a story
to tell you all,
of the mystery of this place."

The Story of St. Anne De Werburg and the Old Grey King

There was a Lady;
she was a princess.
Her name was Anne De Werburg.

Her best friend was
an old grey goose,
and they lived on
the edge of a swamp.

The princess was saintly
and loved her best friend,
but had duties
to reap and sow.

The fields with the
making of flax
for mankind that
began with the elder folk.

Now the princess she had
a faithful friend,
a farmer who worked
in the fields.

Then one night at the
dawn of the year
he was sowing
the seeds of the flax.

When the geese grew so hungry
that they ate all the seeds,
then flew away over the land.

The farmer, so furious,
captured the geese.
But the Old Grey King said,
"I give myself up for my friends."

So, the farmer he took
the old Grey Goose
and made a special feast;
a goose for the field and a glass of wine.

As the day dawned
St. Werburg called out
for the Old Grey King.
But could hear no sound,
from the Bruc or the Dun.
So, she looked far and wide
for her friend.

The farmer was sowing
out in the fields,
when Werburg saw him there.

"Where is the Old Grey King?"
She asked, so scared.
And the farmer replied,
"I ate him in a pie."

Anne of Werburg was furious
And said, "Did you bury the bones?"

"No." said the farmer.
So, she said, "Bring them to me."

Then they took the bones
and bound them together
with mud and paste,
from the edge of the marsh.
Then they buried the goose in the ground.

Then that night as the
moon shone bright
and glowed its special light,
the spirit of Mr. Old Grey Goose,
King of the Gosling line,
stepped out from the
burial mound—

To wander across
the Brooks and the fen
to see Ann Werburg again.

The audience clapped,
cheered, and roared,
then drunk a round of mead.

And the Old Grey King stepped forth
to tell the tale of mystery memes.

The Making of Flax Legend

"Once upon a time,
there was a man who lived
in the hills and the dales.

Herding the cattle,
the goats and the sheep,
he stepped up
over the mound.

With a bow and arrow,
he hunted for food,
as the birds crowed
and called his name.

There on the edge
of the mountainside,
a dark cavern opened up.

He heard the echo of
his name from within
as the crows flew
into the depths.

Then a beautiful stream
flowed over the hill,
as the farmer took a drink.

Then he followed its path
into the hills,
where the cavern was
adorned with ice statues,
and the crows called
the name of the man.

And there stood a lady
shining like a star,
dressed in silver and gold.
She spoke of the
mysteries of life itself
and offered a drink from a jar.

Then she offered
two choices fine,
a sweet blue flower
or a crystal stone.
That the hunter must
herd in the fields.

"Make your choice,
my fine man," said the Lady.

So, the shepherd he took
the blue flax flower.
Then left for his family,
who lived in the vale,
near the village and a town.

He gave the flax
to his wife as a gift
and she watered them in a vase.

Then deep in the night
she had a dream,
that the children would
plant the flowers.

In the morning there was
a basket of seeds sitting
next to the flax flower vase.

So, the wife of the herder
took the basket to the fields
and sowed the seeds in the ground.

The White Lady Bertha
brought many dreams
to the man and his wife,
to reap and sow on the ground.

And they ploughed the fields
and sold the seeds.
Spun and wove, bleaching the linen cloth.

Then their family grew
with many children,
who worked out in all the fields.

Then one day when
he grew so old,
the farmer looked at the vase
and saw the blue flax
fading away.

He ran to see Bertha
the White Lady
in the cave upon the hills.

And she told him the secret
of her flax flowers gift.
That they would live
till the end of his days.

So, she offered him
a home in the cave,
where he lived,
for the rest of his life.

And this is the story
of the Making of Flax,
that brought food
and clothing to mankind.

Yule Tide Feast

The children they clapped
and skipped around,
so happy to hear the lore.

And a great feast ensued
in the mystical cave,
as songs were sung
and mead was made.

Then each presented
their sewing work,
with spindles to Bertha.

Those who had made
a beautiful gown
were gifted with
spindles of gold.

But those who had not
sewed a stitch,
had the spindles
broken and torn,
tossed on the ground,
and turned around.

Then Bertha called Flora forth
to be crowned as
Princess of the Gosling line,
and as the best spinner
at this seasonal time.

Woden stepped forth and called,
"Bring in the Feast!"

And the Boar's head was
brought in on a plate.

The dancing and feasting
lasted all through the night,
as all did misbehave.

Let us leave you there in
the time between time,
in the grotto of sweet Sataere.

For Mrs. Elder and Bertha
the White Lady are
the mother of all life on Earth.

"Greetings, fair ones.
We send you our blessing.
As Mother's Night is
the rebirth of the Sun
and with that said
our work is done.

We wish you Yuletide Greetings.
Merry Christmas,
and a Merry Mother's night."

Notes

1. Trisantoris is the Roman name for the Arun River that flows from St. Leonard's Forest near Horsham. Translated into modern English this means "three times passing." It was also known as Trespasser in local lore.

2. Stempo is a Bavarian version of the Goddess Holda who is mentioned in *Teutonic Mythology*, Volume 1, by Jacob Grimm. He is described as being a giant in Grimm's tale. It features a Midwinter or Christmas legend to encourage children to behave or else Stempo will stomp on them. There is a similar version of Santa Claus in the Sami Indigenous peoples' tradition "Stallu" who will punish naughty children on Solstice morning.

3. The Knucker Dragon swims all the way down Trespasser to the pool beside the hill at the brooks or marshes. Then a fight between St. Leonard brings thunder and lightning, a storm, and a flood over the land which creates the lake from which Goose Island is born. This is a pageant version of the making of Goose Island.

4. Bright Elf Beam is the Sun, an early form of a deity. She has heard of Mrs. Elder's house and knocks on the door to ask for a place to sleep. This brings in the "time between time." This refers to the solstice which lasts three days in the Midwinter during which the sun is static. The dark and light lasts the same length of time during each of these three days. It was seen as a magical time during the pre-Christian era.

5. The Huldra folk plough the land creating an island which was made from the flood. The island is the otherworld. The making of the island, the flood legend, is also the creation of life legend. The meaning of these Midwinter myths and legends in pre-Christian times as in the rebirth of life with the rebirth of the Sun. The Huldra Folk are from the Swedish aspect of Holda, known as Huldra. The island the legend is based on is Sjaelland in Denmark.

6. Vrau Elderstraat (Mrs. Elder Street) is the name for the Milky Way in the Netherlands. Mrs. Elder is a weather and sky deity. Hence the connection to stars.

7. The Heimchen are spirit beings like orphan fairies. This is her "infant train" who follow the wagon as they walk the land,

until they find the abandoned shoe which they move into and make it into a house.

8. Mother's Night, or the Night of the Mothers, is the Night before Christmas Day. It is also the last of the three static days during Solstice. On Christmas Day the daylight will increase by approximately one minute. This phenomenon inspired the pre-Christian belief that the sun was being reborn on this day and thus the night before was Mother's Night.

9. St. Ann of Werburg is an Anglo-Saxon saint and princess whose feast day is February the third. She founded nunneries in three counties including Weedon, Northamptonshire. There is a legend connecting her to a goose set in Chester, Cheshire and Weedon, Northamptonshire written by Goscelin of Saint Bertin in 1095. In the Anglo-Saxon Chronicles kings are often referred to as also being "Woden". In the Golden era in Norse-Germanic culture there were queens and kings who were referred to as also being deities. For example, Skiald a Swedish queen was also believed to be Freyja the great Norse goddess. I found this legend in *The Lore of the Land: A Guide to England's Legends*, by Westwood and Simpson (Penguin) which I have interpreted as being the English version of Holda.

10. The Making of Flax is a legend from the Tyrol in Germany. The Lady featured in the story is one of the many aspects of Holda from North-West Germanic parts of Europe.

L - #0417 - 070323 - C0 - 229/152/4 - PB - DID3515490